Dragon's Pearl

WENDY TARASOFF

DEDICATION

This book is dedicated to children and parents everywhere, and my own family—Christine, Daniel, Jennifer, Jordan, and Talina.

CONTENTS

CONTENTS

DRAGON'S PEARL

ACKNOWLEDGMENTS

I would like to acknowledge others who helped me to read and to write both as a child and later as a university student. No one lives life alone; so, I wish to thank all that have helped me to achieve this goal of writing this book.

To those that love the imagination, my fellow writers who have left behind their words for us to follow in their tracks.

DRAGON'S PEARL

1

"Made of stardust a dragon's pearl has all the elements of the known and the unknown universes and things, magical as all hell too.

"Those who have the precious dragon's pearl age more slowly and are in good spirits. Some of us decide we wish to become dragons. Ever fewer still become a dragon's pearl itself.

"A dragon's pearl can travel on light and enter our solar system with ease, but why one would want to do so is beyond me.

"We, humans and other creatures of Earth, are a strange lot."

Grandy

OFFORON

2

On a dry western slope, lightning ran an outline along a ridge in the darkness.

The dragon Tor flew down the ridge into the cavernous mouth of Dragon Mountain, and landed inside. Using his claws, Tor scraped along a lava-formed floor. Electricity in the air, and lightning from the ridge, had followed him in, winding its way through the cold air into a white dragon's pearl. "They come from the North, 1,000 Gurs strong," said Tor.

The giant, white dragon's pearl, Offoron asked, "The others. The humans? What's their number?"

"...35, maybe 40 have the sight and hear us."

"We'll need their help and that of the little ones, said Offoron."

"The little ones are never called," said Tor, raising his wings up in protest.

"This time they will be." Colors raced and swirled in Offoron and sparks of anger flew out of him. "So few choices left. Does the boy with the curly dark hair and blue eyes know?"

"Daniel, you mean. He is with Grandy right now."

ZORTECK

3

Daniel had a land, Zorteck, a world near Negus Prime. He dreamed about it every night.

Sometimes in nightmares, sometimes in fairy tales, sometimes in it he awoke, certain it was *real*. Difficult to think during schoolwork, Daniel drew many dragons, ones with wings, especially with leathery scaly skin like Tor, and pictures of dragon's pearls both big and small like Offoron made of stardust that contained all the lore of the dragons.

Daniel tried to look through a dragon's eyes to *see what he could see.* Last night he dreamed of Tor, Offoron, and the Gurs.

The Gurs were a bad sort--created chaos. Negus, their leader, was a black pearl. They lived on Negus Prime, Zorteck's first moon. He'd seen Tor and Offoron go to war against them before....

So many dragons blew fire and lost their sparks. Lost in the dark. Lost in the fog of magic. Dead when they hit the ground in either place. Sometimes a wizard could help a dragon to live. (A child might be able to help too if he or she could find a real dragon's pearl.)

Daniel didn't like it one bit, losing his favorite dragons.

The Gurs were growing in numbers. There were so few dragons left.

He *so* loved the dragons of Zorteck, and he *so* loved horses too because he rode one to Zorteck in his dreams.

"Daniel, it's time for bed," said his Grandy.

"Tell me the one about the she horse, Neighs," replied Daniel.

And Grandy spoke aloud:

Neighs

The flying horse, head high,
rides into the night;
hooves across the ground.

Away, she goes, away.

The horse, she Neighs;
stops at your door;
asks you to come,
feet off the floor.

Away, you go, away.

Journey, just the two of you,
to magic land of lands,
past time and sands.

A magic ride, so not a peep.
Now go to bed; get some sleep.

Grandy tucked Daniel into bed, and he lay there trying not to
close his eyes. Finally, he fell asleep.

ZORTECK DREAMING

4

When blue-eyed Daniel woke up in Zorteck, during the time he was supposed to be dreaming, a blue moon was so full its light touched the ground through the forest on a summer's night.

He saw Tor with his mate, Sara dragon, and he walked towards them through the grass. In a nest, he saw six speckled eggs. Some of the brown eggs were hatching. One, two, three so far with little green wings and wee little squeaks and a squawk. Sara and Tor were crying.

"We'll have to find children to love them," sniffed Sara. "And the fairies will have to make small dragon's pearls from Offoron, so the children can have the sight and hear us. Even the Gurs."

"The Gurs are coming," said Tor. "Offoron says--"

"I know, Tor, tonight can't we not speak of the Gurs?"

Little pink trumpet flowers sounded throughout the forest. Magical creatures started arriving--a wizard, a few fairies, two owls, a silver wolf and a rabbit.

"Well now," remarked the wizard Sam, "How do you do, Daniel?"

"How are you?" wooed the owls. "Council tomorrow. Everyone's invited," they said in unison.

"Naming ceremony when it is time," whiskered the black rabbit.

And the wolf growled and pawed at the ground, "Gur...hell of a season to start a family...."

A gray fox trotted on by, but didn't stop to talk. Instead, he carried the news to other creatures in the forest.

Fairies flew about quickly, high up in the air and right

underneath Tor and Sara's nostrils, carrying little blue buckets to catch the dragon tears. One fairy stopped, hovered, and hummed its wings really fast, explaining to Daniel that the tears were magical. "Fairies make four-leafed clovers out of them for one thing for luck, creating secret magical pathways leading to a new fairy hill, and fairy fog to ward off enemies for another."

Sam walked to the top of the new clover fairy hill and waved his wand, tipping it towards the dragons both big and wee. He gave the command, "Orb alight." Green and gold sparks flew from the wand and made an clear orb like a bubble. The orb, dragons and wee ones inside it, floated up and into his right hand. Sam walked off into the fog....

"Daniel? Daniel. Wake up. Time for school," said Grandy. "Let's go."

Daniel was tired when he got up that morning. He had witnessed the birth of baby green dragons and he was worried for them.

Sam would take care of them, wouldn't he? Make sure the Gurs didn't get them? And what about this Council meeting?

Sounds like all the dragons and all the creatures of Zorteck will be there.

What were they going to do about the Gurs? Where was Sam taking the orb?

ALFRED AND THE PASSWORD

5

Daniel was fast asleep in bed, but on Zorteck it was dawn when Neighs, pulling in her white feathery wings, landed in a field.

The morning had streamed over the land in lemony light, and Daniel dreamed again of the mountain cave's mouth high above where Tor went to speak with Offoron about the Gurs. Negus Prime their home world's moon was at quarter shine higher than the trees of Zorteck.

Daniel had the black rabbit on his lap fast asleep, snoring, and just above his right hand a small dragon's pearl glowed and hovered with sparkled stars on its surface. Daniel then held onto it tightly in his hand.

The air was still cold, and Daniel could see his breath. He shivered all over, especially his hands. His pajamas had changed into his long johns and were covered with his favorite clothes and a jacket from home.

A small creek gurgled nearby. A strange feathered bird with a pointy beak perched itself in a tree with bony fingers at the ends of its two, large, bat-like wings. The bird just perched there on a branch with one eye open.

Still on horseback, Daniel asked Neighs to kneel down and let him off. The soft, warm, rabbit woke up in his arms when Daniel landed on firm ground.

"The bird is a keeper of passwords. He will fly down and whisper it in your ear. Don't forget it," said the rabbit. "We have to keep the Gurs out of Council chambers."

Daniel went over and shook the tree. The bird, hanging on with both sets of fingers, opened both eyes and just looked at him. "What do you want?"

"Password."

"Show me your pearl."

"Don't," said the rabbit. "He won't give it back."

"He won't?"

"Nope," said the bird. He shut one eye, looking at Daniel with the other.

"*Pass*word!" said the rabbit.

"Please," said Daniel.

"How do I know if you are a Gur, then, hum?"

"Because I'm not!" Daniel said without speaking.

"You talk our language, human, the password is, and the bird whispered, '*Crombee*', and turned his back to Daniel about to fly off.

"Now Daniel, grab onto his tail feathers, quick."

Daniel did. The bird dragged him several feet before it took to the air. Daniel pulled hard with both hands. He pulled out two tail feathers.

"And a word of warning," crowed the bird, "It will come for you...." The bird pointed to Daniel with a bony finger. "Dead. You hear me." The bird closed one eye, perched himself in the tree, and crowed in a wounded way.

"Don't imagine your worst fear, Daniel, or he'll be right. That bird sees things we can't even imagine, and knows more about the Gurs than anyone of Zorteck."

"What's his name?"

"Herman," said the black rabbit. "Hand me the feathers." He put them into a leather pouch which he then gave to Daniel.

"And your name?"

"Alfred. And I already have my password. Let's go."

Alfred grew legs, hind legs, with paws. He walked beside Daniel on and on and off into a bank of fairy fog. Neighs flew in the air above them as if she knew exactly where they were all of the time.

"And a word of warning," crowed the bird, "It will come for

you...." The bird pointed to Daniel with a bony finger. "Dead. You hear me." The bird closed one eye, perched himself in the tree, and crowed in a wounded way.

"Don't imagine your worst fear, Daniel, or he'll be right. That bird sees things we can't even imagine, and knows more about the Gurs than anyone of Zorteck."

"If you have just been here before, you have," said Alfred. *"Time warp."*

"What?"

"We need your help, Daniel."

BLACK RABBIT

6

Daniel arrived at school to find a small black rabbit in a cage. He looked at the rabbit eating a carrot, and the rabbit looked at him and said, "What are you looking at?"

Daniel took a step back.

The rabbit's nose wriggled up and he said, "Sh--"

Daniel glanced around at the other students watching, and the rabbit said to him, "Hey, I'm from Zorteck, and this is the dumbest thing I've ever had to do for a human. In English. Captive. With all those poking fingers."

What are you doing here...? Daniel thought.

Because you couldn't come by horse, silly. They can't hear me, you know. You have been given a small pearl from Zorteck, child, and I'm here, just now. So listen up. You are to visit with the Wizard Sam at the Cobalt Cave before Council. Got that?"

"Yes...but I--"

Fellow students turned to look at him, "Who are you talking to?"

"The rabbit."

Giggles all the way around.

"But he said--"

"Yes, I did," said the rabbit. *Ears on, you. Pay attention in your daydream this morning during English Class.* With that, the rabbit just kept on munching.

VISIT WITH A WIZARD

7

Daniel found himself later that morning thinking about the rabbit and Zorteck, and wishing that he could go there. Some subjects like English were a bit difficult for Daniel, but he kept trying to get what his teacher was saying. The room started to swirl a bit and the walls changed into trees. The desks became a pathway leading to a rocky cave with vines climbing around the outside.

A voice in the cave echoed out, "Bring your imagination. Come in. Sit there," and a stool appeared nearby.

Seated, Daniel watched a table take shape like a workbench. On the knotted wood stood some glass bottles, different sizes and colors. He read some of the labels: "Wiggleworts" (eyes blinked in there, lots of them with pairs of lips), and "Snoots"? "Wiggleworts," said Daniel unscrewing the lid, reaching inside.

Whatever they were, they were sticky. He pulled one out and it grew bigger. Another flew out and did the same thing. Both smacked their lips together and said, "Who's he?" Their eyes grew wider, looking hungry. They had no teeth! That was a good sign, wasn't it?

More kept coming out of the bottle, pouring out. Lips surrounded him. He stood up from the stool thinking maybe it was time to run.

The wiggleworts flew through the air and attached themselves to his butt. Daniel shrieked. He tried to pull one off, but it was stuck there, and it screeched back at him.

In the distance, there was laughter and it got closer and closer, louder and louder. "Daniel," said the Wizard Sam now standing beside him, "Laugh!"

"I don't think this is very funny," said Daniel, showing his butt to the wizard.

"Laugh. Wiggleworts fall off when you do that."

Daniel wasn't so sure, so he tried to laugh and then he laughed harder and harder and harder. When Daniel doubled over with laugher, the wiggleworts fell off one by one.

"Now imagine them back in the bottle."

Daniel did, and there were no more wiggleworts floating around making any more noise. The lid flew back on and turned itself shut. He wasn't a wizard like Sam. He didn't have a wand, so what had happened?

"Possible only happens when you imagine, Daniel. Imagination comes down to making something real over time. What you thought was in the bottle was in the bottle. That's lesson number one. Return to school."

Daniel was back in his classroom. The rabbit was gone. The cage was too. His teacher never missed him. She was still talking about English. He sat there thinking.... How is it that I never left, yet I was not here.

Imagination, Daniel realized, was a powerful thing. Maybe it's the best thing in the *whole* world!

Daniel had put the wiggleworts back into the bottle all by himself. How did he do that? Was it the small dragon's pearl from Zorteck that helped him do it? He shook the idea off. The idea fell on the floor, and eyes looked back at him. *Oh, no, not again.*

He had problems to solve in life, in Zorteck too, and he decided he would do what he could do. Some daydream! What could his future hold if he could create it just like that? Wiggleworts, Daniel giggled, to himself. He felt something soft in his hands, and looked down. There was the black rabbit curled up in his hands, sleeping.

DRAGON MOUNTAIN

8

Out of the fog Neighs landed, and Daniel and Alfred arrived at the bottom of the Dragon Mountain by midday where they reached a tall magic gate with two golden dragon eyes on it. The eyebrows moved up and then narrowed; slitted-eyes opened wide and stared right at them, through them.

Daniel thought, *he sees me*.

"Right you are. Daniel, Alfred?" A voice boomed. Dragon eyes blinked on the dragon's gate. "Alfred?"

"Yes."

"Show the young lad something about his dragon's pearl for entry."

Alfred let his dragon's pearl hover above his paw. The pearl lit up clear white with an eyeball blinking in it. Clearly now an image formed of dragon's eyes. "Now, say your password, but not out loud."

Daniel opened his right hand, and his dragon's pearl hovered. "This is too easy." He whispered to himself, *Crombee*. Nothing would happen, right? Wrong. Razor sharp talons reached out for Daniel.

"You forgot to summon the gate," said Alfred.

The talons were almost to his head. "Oh!" said Daniel. Yellow eyes appeared. Terrible eyes in the pearl. "Oh, no."

"Don't even think any of it," Alfred said. "Look at the dragon eyes on the gate."

Daniel had the eyes swirling in his dragon's pearl.

"Daniel, don't make me dizzy. Stop, okay? Say the password,"

"Oh, my!" said Alfred. He pulled one of Herman's bird feathers from his leathery pouch, and waved it over his pearl as a dragon's nose appeared in front of the gate. The dragon's nose on the gate sneezed.

Alfred now had a small bucket in his paws and caught most of the dragon's sneeze in the bucket, and off into the pouch everything went. The bucket with a lid on it too.

Crombee....

Daniel and Alfred walked past the gate through a wall of fire, and stood on a spiral staircase. Cool and dark, the pearls shone light into the empty places where Daniel and Alfred's shadows were followed along by echoing steps.

Up they walked while Alfred explained, "These steps were built out of solid stone, and lead up to spiral balconies built inside the mountain. Dragon Mountain moves and is never in the same place on Zorteck. This is for our protection from an attack. Gurs." Alfred shivered, "...and their shadows."

"Yeow!" yelled out Daniel, opening his eyes. He had almost been set on fire by a dragon's breath, his hair and all.

He was so hot to the touch, his pants were burning his skin. He jumped around his room.

"Yes," answered Grandy from downstairs, "Be careful at the top of the stairs."

Daniel opened his hand, and there was the dragon's pearl hovering. "Zorteck is real," he whispered.

"Of course it is," said Alfred. "You made it through to council chambers. So few do, you know. Three others have made it from your world this time, and one adult."

Neighs was there too galloping about over his bed.

ENGLISH CLASS, DRAGON CLASS

9

The next day, Daniel was returning to his desk in English class when he noticed a peculiar thing.

Alfred was sitting on his desktop looking like his regular, sleepy self, and there were three other rabbits sleeping on the laps of three other students.

Lindy, Jake, and Harry were there, staring at their rabbits, watching Daniel go to his desk to ask Alfred what was going on.

"Alfred?"

Snore.

"Alfred--" said Daniel.

"Why yes," said Alfred, "POOF," went his magical dragon's pearl in his paws, lights and colors swirling.

Offoron, the giant pearl, spoke through Alfred's pearl, "Welcome new Zorteck Dragons. To the rest of you, the dragon's pearls you hold are little baby ones of me."

Light shone over the rabbits with such brilliance, and stars moved from the light along with whole galaxies back into the pearl that Alfred held.

Lindy, Jake, and Harry each had a dragon's pearl like Daniel's, swirling with colors.

Offoron arrived in the classroom, getting bigger and bigger.

From the door of the classroom, a layer of fog moved around Offoron as if he were on a mountaintop.

Out of the fog, stepped Wizard Sam with his orb. The dragon family still inside.

Sam stood in front of the class with the teacher, Ms. Collins.

"Orb release," called out Sam. The orb grew bigger and bigger. Tor, Sara, and three baby dragons were all their normal size again.

The three baby dragons moved beside the desks of the children. On the floor, the dragons' claws caught up in the carpet. They tripped forward. Their heads crashed to the floor with a muffled thud.

Nobody else heard them at all, even their squeaks and squawks.

However, Lindy, and Jake, and Harry said, "Oh...! Rabbits...Dragons."

Nobody heard them except either Daniel or Alfred, or so Daniel thought.

Their teacher, Ms. Collins, then called them into a group. "You have an extra lesson today in order to start your dragon training. Pat your dragon to make him or her feel better; get your dragon to stand upright without falling on the carpet again, and learn to speak with your dragon."

The children all gasped as the fog cleared the room.

Sam said, "The teacher has a lot to teach today, Daniel, so do I. Council is this evening and the Gurs are getting too close. Have to be ready."

"Are you a dragon too?" Daniel asked Alfred. "Where's my dragon?"

"I'm special; I am any form you can imagine, Daniel, including a dragon."

Alfred continued, "The others are small yet and can only do two of the forms you see, rabbit and dragon. They must practice to become good at all forms and you must help them. Practice your forms."

Ms. Collins added, "Much to be done ahead of you. You are all special too."

Offoron hovered over Tor's dragon-tail. Inside Offoron was a picture of Dragon Mountain. Beautiful shades of crimson were in the sky. It was near nightfall on Zorteck.

For the first time the children could see a Gur, a lot of Gurs walking towards dragon mountain. Covered in fur, and with big sharp teeth and bulgy eyes. None of them looked friendly. They had very long dark shadows that followed them, the blackest of black.

Daniel watched as the other children were speaking to their dragons.

The dragon's pearls, acting like translators between two very different worlds, vibrated with sounds, and the dragons were trying to learn English, a task difficult even for an adult dragon.

Fairies showed up to collect a few baby dragon tears.

Daniel feared none of them would be hearing good news about the Gurs that was for sure. Could he save Dragon Mountain?

BABY GUR, BARTH

10

From black and trouble,
boiled round the rim,
cauldron's fire through none,
no mortals swim.

It was a foggy night. Lindy, Jake, Harry, and Daniel began
meeting in their dreams...deep into a world of water and black,
the water swirled and bubbled up, lapping over into a red sky.
The four children met on a craggy rock looking out over a molten
lava lake. On a rock sat a boiling cauldron.

"We are not on Zorteck, are we?" asked Lindy. "Neighs isn't
here."

Alfred showed up too. "No, you are on Negus Prime."

Daniel, Jake and Harry moved toward the cauldron to look
inside.

Jagged teeth snarled out of it in a black, dripping, mass. It
gurred and growled and howled as if in great pain. Rising out of
the goop and out of the iron cauldron, a Gur planted itself in the
ash.

"This baby Gur," said Alfred, "is made of dragon's teeth, and
will form an army against Zorteck."

"Do they breath fire?" asked Jake.

"Or Ice?" asked Harry.

"What happens if they get a dragon's pearl?" Daniel said
worriedly.

"Yes," said Alfred to all three of them. "A dragon's pearl is the wisdom of the beginning of time and contains all dragon-lore. It must be protected knowledge. Your pearls are at the beginning levels, so not much harm can come, but as you move up in understandings, the more you have power, the greater the responsibility."

"Can a Gur change form like you can?" asked Daniel of Alfred.

Alfred didn't answer. Instead his pearl hovered over his dragon-form, golden and translucent. He called for the other one-year-old dragons to come. "You will become one with your dragon by flying above the Gurs, and by teaching your dragon to flame fire."

Three green dragons flew towards them, swooping against the red sky. Circling westward, they soared like they could touch the descending sun. They landed nearby. Each had a saddle on it ready to ride.

The dragons laid down to let the children on, and up the other children went, wing after wing beating into the air.

Daniel was still on the ground with Alfred. "You are not like the other dragons. You're a metallic dragon, one that honors truth above all else."

"And you will lead the others with me, and are held to the highest of standards, Daniel. I am your mentor: You could be my apprentice."

Into the air they winged. Daniel gripped the golden scales against his thighs. The rainbow colors on each scale were lined in gold layers.

Alfred's dragon breath roared outward in ribbons of fire. He dove for some Gurs whose feet were coming out of the ground. Then nothing was left but a few footprints on the soil. Not even a skeleton remained.

Daniel called out, "No.... STOP."

The green dragons followed with more fire flames. It looked as if Lindy was having trouble, and through their dragon's pearls they saw her dragon needed to breathe more deeply in order to aim fire at the Gurs. He took deeper and deeper breaths. Smoke billowed out, then blazing fire.

Jake and Harry's dragons had done their first dive towards some Gurs walking in a group, but this time the Gurs were ready and spewed back fire at them. Jake and Harry had to regroup and try again.

Harry's dragon did a dive and got some Gurs reduced to nothing at all.

When it was all over, there were no more dragon's teeth or Gurs in the ash or walking towards Zorteck. The cauldron was almost empty. One more baby Gur jumped out of the cauldron and planted itself in the ash.

Daniel made Alfred dive down and land next to the baby to talk with it.

"Hello," said Daniel to the Gur. Daniel hugged the ugly baby Gur.

"Why would you hug me?" it said, walking out of the ash and blowing fire over Daniel's shoulder.

Daniel replied, "Because I love you."

"Me? I don't want to spew fire, but I was made--" The baby Gur was crying river of water and ash.

"Alfred, where is the feather we have from the strange bird...Herman? Can you get it from your pouch?"

"I don't think this is a good idea, Daniel," said Alfred.

"We have two magic feathers, Alfred. He can have one."

"What's your name," said Daniel to the Gur.

"Barth."

"Okay, Barth. We are friends now. When you wave this feather, I will see it in my dragon's pearl and find you if you call."

"It's not okay to kill," said Daniel to Alfred and Barth. "It's not okay to rain down fire from above or blow it up from below."

The cauldron bubbled and boiled angrily. "The evil dragon's pearl that has no light in it, Negus, has bigger Gurs on the horizon. Some of those with him have sat in their council chambers in private doing evil instead of good to many. If they ask you to kill, will you do it?" Daniel asked the baby Gur.

"No, I won't do it! I won't."

"It is our secret, then," said Daniel.

It's time to go," said Alfred. "There are bigger Gurs yet. The day will come when you are ready. Some will be dragons; some will be human. You may or may not be able to befriend them all."

Daniel, Lindy, Jake, and Harry were back in their beds. Daniel heard Alfred say to the other dragons, "Return to the Zorteck lair at Dragon Mountain by midnight."

"It's not right, Alfred."

"No, it's not. This is but a dream, Daniel, nothing more. "You have passed the first of many tests."

"If you truly are an apprentice of mine, then you will be a true leader. You have learned the first lesson of wisdom…do not slay or rain down fire just because you are asked to. The baby Gur could be your friend, or neighbor, who has done you or others no harm." Alfred disappeared into some fairy fog. "Good night, Daniel."

Daniel slept fitfully turning this way and that. He couldn't escape from the black waters he felt and saw. Teeth were trying to pull him underneath, yet he managed to stay afloat. He cried for help to Grandy, and she came to his bedside. He tried to explain.

Grandy listened and loved him until he fell asleep again.

INSIDE DRAGON MOUNTAIN

11

Daydreams played with the light between trees, and all of a sudden the trees were gone. Daniel and the others were in the park after school, and then they weren't. They were at the bottom of a rock spiral staircase, their pants too hot to touch.

Alfred met them there. Each pulled out their dragon's pearl made of stardust, glowing in the darkness; up the stairs they climbed.

"The stairs are hollowed out where we step," said Lindy. "How many others have been here before us?"

"The dust smells ancient," said Harry.

And Jake just held onto Alfred's other paw.

Alfred finally spoke, "We're to go all the way to the top of the Dragon Mountain, and then you are to listen much."

There were echoes of a great number of voices around the curves of lava rock. At the top of the staircase, the circular ceiling still vaulted above them like a dragon egg.

Dusty moonlight filled the whole inside of the mountain. The children looked below and gasped. There was a circular room, and Offoron hovered in the center. To the left was the strange bird, Herman, sitting in his tree with one eye closed, and then there were the dragons Tor and Sara.

Alfred found a place for Lindy, Jake, Harry and Daniel next to the rock railing, then disappeared and reappeared in the Council Chamber with Offoron.

The noise in the chamber was deafening.

"There is Neighs with the other horses!" yelled Harry.

"Goblins!" said Jake.

"Spiders with big eyes," said Lindy,"...snakes, oh I hate them."

One the long snakes looked over at her fiercely.

"Some are human; some have dragon's pearls like ours. Most do not," said Daniel. "There are so many here. Even Sam the Wizard."

It got really quiet and still as Sam raised his magic wand. Fairy fog filled the chamber, a wolf howled. When the fog lifted, there were wee baby dragons just hatched and fully grown dragons of all different colors, green, red, blue, brass, gold.

And Herman crowed, "The Gurs are coming. We have little time to prepare for an attack. Even the wee ones of every kind will be needed to save Zorteck, each at his level of understanding of our ways."

Offoron added, "The new humans partnered with the one-year-old green dragons yesterday to destroy the new Gurs, but 1,000 Gurs with much more power are coming."

Sam raised his wand to Offoron and there was a picture of the Gurs burning down the border villages. Some of the villagers were pleading with the Gurs to spare them and their property; most died by fire or by snarling teeth.

Daniel looked at Lindy worriedly.

Jake turned to Harry, "They have more than fire. What else? How are we to help?"

Alfred calmed everyone down. "You will work in groups of three or four with Tor and Sara and Alfred. Not to fear. That'll do the least good. Remember, your worst fear is what they feed on and today the Gurs will grow in numbers if you let them."

Daniel remembered the sharp talons had come for him when he was at the dragon gate. He felt fear, and in his pearl he could see the sharp teeth and the bulgy eyes and something else--a black dragon's pearl. It had no light in it. None at all. And a voice echoed, "I know who you are...."

Offoron answered back, "None of my dragons and friends are afraid of you--Negus."

Wild yawls and sniping Gurs voices rose within the black pearl, "Get you yet. Zorteck is ours."

TESTS AND SOUL HEARTS

12

"Tests, more tests," said Daniel. "Tell me why?"

"We've got to get back in for school," urged Lindy.

"I tried to put a spell on my dragon's pearl so I can cheat," said Harry walking along beside them.

"No way!" said Jake pulling up his pants, "Did it work?"

"No such luck. Tora and Sara and Alfred just stared back at me in the pearl, and I got a jolt of lightning 'round the pearl into my hand. The pearl whizzed around me and into my pocket: Haven't been able to dig it out since," said Harry sliding into his desk chair.

Ms. Collins announced, "Yes, English Test. The test is on the word 'Focus'. Hear what it means in Latin (L.): 'Focus'- a point where light-rays meet L. 'Focus', a hearth; a center of fire.

"Write a two paragraph story on what 'Focus' means to you." Handing out page details to each student she promptly added, "10 minutes."

Daniel started to write with his ordinary pen when he noticed a magic pen and piece of paper had come out of his dragon's pearl. He closed his eyes and asked, "Pearl? Tell me of a dragon's heart?"

"Each dragon's heart is one of a kind and must match the apprentice's heart."

"Tell me of Alfred's."

"Nope, your heart must have the same fiery focus. Tell Alfred a story about your heart, and I will write what you have written there. Know that you cannot lie to me or to yourself."

I am a little boy with big dreams. I want love. I deserve love from others. But especially I want to love myself with a fiery focus from my heart to the outside world.

I want light in my world not darkness. Is there a dragon that has the same heart of fire, the same focus that I have? Will we experience riding high on the winds of Zorteck? Can we travel together with a fire so great for life that it overpowers us?

"Alfred will you answer?"

The magic pen wrote, "Yes...I will. Meet me outside after you hand in your paper to Ms. Collins." The words then became invisible on the page.

Daniel went out to the soccer field behind the school. There stood Alfred on his back claws at the other end of the field. Daniel walked towards Alfred with such love that white light emanated from his heart.

Alfred opened up his breastplate to show his heart. Light, so much light, met Daniel's light between them. Daniel's dragon's pearl flew into the center of the light and glowed all the colors of the rainbow. There was a focus, a home place of fire which returned to both their hearts.

"It is done. You have completed the this test, Daniel. We are soul hearts."

DRAGONS

13

The span of wings, the glide of kings, in the wind soar and roar.
Neighs and her kind, pulled in their feathery horse wings, landed
Daniel and the others in the field where Herman sat in his tree
watching with one eye. Alfred, flew to the ground, pushed his
claws into the dirt beside them. He awoke Daniel and the other
children from sleep near dawn.

Daniel's dragon's pearl hovered in his right hand but didn't
leave him. "Look at them all," said Daniel. The air was filled with
dragon's pearls, and dragons everywhere in the air and on the
ground.

The air cracked with the sound of dragons swooping through
the air. "What are they doing?" asked Daniel.

"Hunting!" crowed out Herman, "...soon to begin." Herman had
a pearl scepter with his bony fingers stretched around it. The
scepter struck the ground 3 times and the pearl inside it glowed.
"Begin," he said.

"All the dragons are taking flight," said Lindy looking back at
Harry, Jake, and Daniel.

"The pearls are all alight like Herman's scepter," said Harry
including ours. All the children had their pearls hovering above
their hands.

"Are all these made from Offoron?" Daniel asked Alfred.

"Yes," said Alfred, "this has been done for 1.000 of years.
Offoron is testing each of the dragons of each kind. Come with me
into the air, Daniel." Alfred and Daniel took flight.

It was cold in the air, and they went higher and higher and
circled Zorteck. The light drew together like a star, and the Alfred
dove straight down. The air crackled and thundered with all its

might: Alfred reached his talons forward, and grabbed two pearls each in a talon. The air moved hard against Alfred's beating wings to keep them from hitting the ground. One of his talons went to his mouth, and he swallowed one pearl whole; the other three to his chest where the pearls merged with his breastplate. Alfred landed hard on the ground.

"You have just witnessed my rank. I am a star dragon of dragons because of the height and speed at which I can travel. No human has ever witnessed these events. Now put your dragons pearl to my breast."

Lindy and the others gathered round. A star formed between the breastplate and Daniel's dragon's pearl. Herman's voice questioned, "Do you wish this Alfred. This boy is untrained in our ways."

"I will train him," said Alfred. The star that was in the sky now searched Daniel for any sign of fear, and finding none, seared a small star into his forehead.

Daniel screamed.

Alfred answered, "It is for your protection."

Jake said, "The star--"

"Is invisible," said Lindy, putting her hands to Daniel's forehead, not even a scar.

And Harry was in the air with his dragon climbing higher and higher.

It took most of the day for all the dragons and pearls to join and form the various ranks--ice dragons, green dragons, red dragons, white dragons were all in groups according to rank and talking. Both male and female together they made one last flight into the air in mated pairs. Each pair forming a love-heart in mid-air that appeared to float down to the field until many talons hit the ground in a deafening thrum.

THE MAGIC BOX

14

Alfred was sleeping on the floor. Between his talons lay a large, metal, locked box with a metallic dragon on its top. Daniel touched the box; the dragon on the top blew fire and then puffs of smoke: its tail formed the lock for the box.

Alfred awoke with a start, and then into his rabbit form.

Daniel's eyes scoured Alfred's, looking for answers.

"The box is yours once you become one with the box, Daniel."

"How do I do that?"

Alfred laughed, "You are a star child."

"But how?"

"Put your hand, slowly, over the dragon's nostrils."

"What about the fire?" said Daniel, nervously.

"Feel the fire in your heart and become one with it."

Daniel put his hand on the nostrils of the dragon. His hand was really hot and on fire. He held on. "I am feeling the heat go to my heart."

The dragon's tail started to move like a tumbler clicking and the lock was opened fully. The top of the box slid opened of its own accord.

Daniel peered inside to the dark. It seemed empty.

"Look closer," said Alfred. "The box is light although it looks heavy. You will be able to put it into your pouch. I've been collecting some things in there for you." Daniel's eyes went wild, and Alfred could see the star on his forehead forge a link with the box, and something Daniel grabbed in the darkness squirmed in the box.

Daniel hung on to it, and pulled out a scroll with dragon

language marks, and a golden seal on the outside.

"Unravel!" called out Alfred.

The scroll flew to Daniel's bedroom desk and unrolled.

"Now, Daniel put your hand on the scroll."

Daniel did so and watched a fiery handed print disappear into its surface.

"Only you will be able to read the scroll."

"What's it for?"

"Guidance through the magic realms of fairies, wizards, dragons," said Alfred.

Daniel saw words appear in the center of the scroll. The words were "Dragon's Pearl."

Alfred handed Daniel the pouch.

Daniel felt it wriggle. He opened it and reached inside. In his hands was another dragons pearl, heavier than the first one he had, but different with a star on it.

Alfred looked into Daniel's blue eyes, "Daniel, this is your level one dragons pearl. It rose above Daniel's right hand and rotated there and hummed.

There was a star burst from Daniel's forehead to the pearl, and the scroll then read "Initiation complete."

"Carry the pouch with you with the pearl inside wherever you are including school."

"How do I close the box?" asked Daniel.

"Oh, just touch the tail. The dragon roared more flames, and its tail closed the lock, tightly shut.

Bang! Daniel was back in his room and jumped out of his bed. He found the box on his dresser; the pouch lay beside it.

THE GUR HANDBOOK

15

Daniel opened the magic box and inside a book hovered. The cover read, "Gur Handbook for the Dragon Apprentice." The cover growled and howled when he undid the clasp.

"What are the Gurs?" thought Daniel.

The pages flipped to chapter 1: The Gurs.

In illuminated text that was not there before these words appeared:

"They are of the imagination, too.

"What is meant by that is that they use their imaginations for bad things, like traps and mental paralysis.

"Using fear and emotions to harm others. Although they can walk and talk dragon and human, their main drive is to get you to do things harmful by talking you into doing them thereby using your power as their own, physically or in the mind.

"Their strength is really the shadows of your own. But if you let them use your shadow, they become the power of two or more.

"What does it mean to be scared of your own shadow?"

Then the book went blank.

Shadows, Daniel thought. Fear. He looked at his dragon's pearl, a dark cloud appeared in them. Inside and outside the dark was growing longer shadows into the night.

What do I do? Daniel thought.

The handbook raced ahead.

Words illuminated again, a dragon ring. Inside the box there were four such identical rings, one for each child. Each of the rings was a Mexican Fire Opal with red and blue fames sparking inside it, it sounded with a magical roar of wind. Daniel pulled it out of the box, and it flew onto his right index finger.

Daniel's shadow drew closer to his body and spoke aloud. "I am your guard."

The pearl was as usual again, no dark clouds anywhere noticed Daniel.

"Fear is not something you play with. Fear is deadly. I will help you with the fear that is to come."

Daniel could not move; the shadow did not move. There was a deadly silence in the room. F E A R moved in the room towards him, through him. It kept growing in the sound of a wind climbing around the walls in the room. "The Gurs, I feel them," said Daniel.

"Yes," said the shadow. "Negus."

THE MAP & COMPASS

16

Daniel knew he needed to see that map.

He crawled out of bed, put his hand on the dragon's nose, and inside the box he found it.

Daniel put his whole palm on the map, and the edges glowed, and in the center of the map, a gem glowed bright blue in a golden magic compass. He reached for the gem, and it came out of the compass into his hands. It felt warm and light and hard. The gem had a glint to it like a star with one stream of light that pointed to the right side of the map.

There, where the beam of light touched, an island revealed. The title under the island read Zimbar. Daniel touched the island and it grew in size on the map, and a description read, "Atlantis." He had heard of Atlantis as being from the far, far past of the Grandy's and Alfred's worlds.

He was trying to figure out what it was all about when Alfred appeared on the map with the letter "T" underneath him. When pressing on the "T" a history appeared on the map like a small scroll.

Reading down the map the words said, "Apprentice, you are entering the realm of time where worlds find each other in a rift, a riptide in space and time, and a place where you must repair for whole worlds to survive. Find Alfred and Grandy and travel to Zimbar which on Earth is Atlantis."

The map rolled itself back up and hovered by itself and went back in the magic box. Daniel tried to command it to stop, but it would not listen. It spoke aloud, "Repair."

The magic box closed by itself, and Daniel tried again to open it.

The lock would not budge, and the dragon on top of the box would not move when his nose was touched.

Then the dragon's pearl which was perched by his bed on a shelf began to hum and the compass with the blue gem now inside it disappeared inside the pearl.

"Grandy, Grandy!" Daniel called for her.

"Yes, Daniel?"

"Tell me of Neighs, the magic horse so we both can go to Zorteck. I cannot wait. You must come Grandy. I need you."

In an instant Neighs was there flying over his bed and Daniel was on his way to Zorteck. Daniel closed his eyes and was fast asleep with the dragon's pearl in his hands.

Grandy covered him up with a blanket. Grandy went to bed, a dragon's pearl in her hands too. But Alfred's voice echoed in all of dreamtime, "No, not yet. Wait and sleep. All will gather in the boy's room before the shadows come."

NEGUS

17

The last light at nightfall slid into the darkness of shadows, but Daniel, Lindy, Harry and Jake were in Daniel's bedroom jumping on the bed when a fairy fog bank rolled in and settled around and over the children now seated. (Each child wore their Mexican Fire Opal ring).

Out of the fog came a voice, "Negus wants you all dead," said Offoron.

"That's why the fog," said Alfred. There was a groan and a snap of the bed frame. The bed fell flat to the floor, broken. Pieces of the frame fell out of the fairy fog, and Alfred was in the fog up to his neck, "Sorry, about that. Just forgot I couldn't sit down is all as a dragon," said Alfred. "Forgot to change to rabbit form. Sam will fix it. Sam, where are you?"

The children, looking for Sam, poked their heads out of the fog bank.

"Here by the curtains," said Sam. The curtains were shaking and little pairs of eyes peeked out from there, frightened. Below, little pointy toes curled up on the ends, shaking.

"Fairies come out now and sit in a circle around the children," said Offoron.

The fairies came out from behind the curtains, uncomfortably sitting on the floor, so Sam made mushrooms with pink underbellies for them to sit on with his wand.

The fog rolled off the bed and formed a circle around the fairies too. Everyone could see a bit better. Offoron was hovering pearly beside the bed.

"Now that you are all safe, we can talk," said Offoron. Shadows of Gurs were growling and snapping at the fairy fog on the outside, but inside the circle there was silence.

Daniel worried for Grandy. Did she hear the bed fall? Would the Gurs get her?

"Never mind about Grandy. She's here, too," said Alfred.

Grandy caught Daniel's attention. Grandy was talking to one of the mushrooms asking it to sit up straight for one of the fairies to sit on.

"Grandy is the adult admitted to Dragon Mountain," said Alfred to Daniel and the rest.

"Pull out your dragon's pearl from your pocket," commanded Offoron. "Hold your pearl up to the ceiling. Now look closely inside it with only your right eye. Fairies will stay and guard the room. Alfred you and Grandy are with us and the children."

Time permitted light to bend, and for a time, time could slide into another present. In the in between time, Offoron spoke, "A long time ago, there was a place called Atlantis. Mermaids lived there alongside dragons and dragon's pearls and dolphins.

"Negus and Offoron were there too, as dragon pearls live a long, long, time. Long before that, Negus and Offoron were dragons.

"And before that they were humans like you are. They were humans holding hands on the beach. Another dragon's pearl is being born today whose destiny is in peril. Negus wants the power of that pearl and more.... We go to Zimbar. Look only with the right eye."

Before the children could say 'Where?' Each eye reflected in a pearl blinked and time shifted.

RIPTIDE

18

Dragons soar
And land
On grains of sand
Upon an
Island

The sea in white caps
Roar

Zimbar, Zorteck: It is where Alfred and the other dragons
landed with Daniel, Jake, Harry, Lindy, and Grandy.

White sandy beaches with salty brine and seaweed, rocks
covered in kelp at high noon.

Even the standing salt water in pools was crystal clear light blue
to the bottom. Daniel, Jake, Harry, and Lindy along with Tor and
Sara and and other dragons present could see images of
themselves in the pools of yellow sea horses before them. Grandy
too.

With water wings, the horses must be related to Neighs thought
Daniel, but the horizon out to sea sure looked a bit dark.

The wind picked up and the images in the pools became
unclear. Lindy's hair lifted up and swam around her head and
then down back to her neck. All seemed calm again.

Her eyes almost mesmerized by all that she could see--the
purple rocks, sea birds, giant open clam shells and Daniel.

Their two hands touched.

Then lightning came down from the sky and struck land
nearby, and they held hands. Both Daniel and Lindy startled by

the jolt and the thunder, stood jumpy and on the edge of land and sea, looking towards the incoming storm.

Out in the water, streams of white light bubbled to the surface along with an eerie sound.

"Do you see-hear that?" said Daniel.

Harry answered, "No."

"Looks like fish tails," said Lindy.

Jake said, "I don't see anything, but clouds, bad clouds."

Alfred spoke directly to Daniel, "Two of you have the sight, then. That's for sure. You see what we see and also what we hear. You and Lindy will have to defend. For real, Daniel."

"What?" said Daniel. He held out his dragon's pearl towards the ocean, and so did Lindy.

"What is it Daniel?" said Lindy.

The foam moved forward towards them; rough indigo, dark blue, waves pouring over their feet and heads and hands and fish tails moved onto the beach in the tall spray. Hands reached for Daniel's and Lindy's feet.

"Mermaids," said Daniel. He could see them in his pearl just before he felt their hands on his feet drag him into the ocean.

The lightning struck again down the beach with a boom.

"Daniel, Daniel," cried out Lindy. She was holding on tight to Daniel's hand, but she was being pulled in. Drag marks in sand were being covered by salty brine as if they had never been there.

Daniel held his pearl tightly; Lindy held hers too. For some reason they were floating, bobbing in the sea, being carried in the arms of mermaids.

Both of them could see jagged rocks coming out of the water ahead. It was there that the mermaids put them where they could sit on the stone steps Daniel had felt under his feet to land on. His pearl was underwater in his hand and he saw Lindy's under the crystal clear dark blue ocean.

"Do you hear them, Daniel?" said Lindy. "Please don't let go of my hand."

Screeches above the waves turn to words underneath. "Negus wants them. He's here. Very close. Watch out."

On the beach, Jake and Harry and Grandy are running between lightning flashes where steel chards of dark were ripping through the air and cracking down through the sand like ragged-edged barbed wire. Between the chards, electricity charged and shadows grew. Negus, an all-black dragon's pearl, had arrived floating among the chards.

Daniel and Lindy felt their pearls drawing closer to each other, magnetic, and out of the ocean and up in the air the pearls then floated. Touching, the pearls put out white sparks and then arced back into Daniel and Lindy's hands.

The same was happening on the beach to Jake and Harry and Grandy. Electricity struck each of the pearls, swirling and humming. The darkness was flung off and the light absorbed. Grandy, and Jake and Harry's pearls like orbs flew towards and circled Negus.

Daniel heard Alfred speak quietly in his soul heart, "Ask the mermaids while the three dragon pearls hold off the attack."

Lindy heard it too in her soul heart. They looked at each other shocked.

Daniel looked at the nearest mermaid, "Are you with Negus or with us?" The waves were roaring close to a riptide. Soon Daniel felt they would both be dragged underneath.

Daniel and Lindy put their pearls touching under the ocean waves, and asked again, "Will you help us?" into the white water caps and roaring ocean.

"Help us, Daniel and Lindy. Negus wants more power. The power to move out of shadow even in the sea. He wants what we guard," said the mermaids in one voice.

From under the waves, the mermaids brought forth a trident. It took everything they had to hold part of it above the salt water. The trident had three prongs and a large hole in the center for a dragons pearl, and the trident was pulled back under the water. Daniel and Lindy noted that whatever was supposed to be in the center was missing.

The dragon's pearl... Alfred said to Daniel from his soul heart.

"Where is it?" asked Daniel.

One of the mermaids answered, "It is being born in the sea under your feet. That is what is causing the water to riptide."

On the beach, Negus was hovering in the air. On the ground, some of the shadows were taking Gur shapes, dragon ugly with sharp teeth, and some where spewing fire.

In the air, Grandy and the other children on dragons were spewing fire back.

So far the three dragon's pearls combined were holding Negus on the beach, but not for long.

Add to this fact, fog was rolling over the sea making it hard to see what was happening.

Some of the Gurs were gliding in the air on wings headed straight for where the trident was last seen. They were drawn to it and the mermaids were doing all they could to keep the trident below the water because one said, "It will rise as the pearl rises. The two must go together to stop the riptide of time and space."

The ocean was doing all it could to whirl and whiz into a spinning pool. At the center of the blue water, a pearl was moving up from the depths casting aside its rippled clam shell. The pearl hovered over the water now, the riptide slowing down. Along with it rose the trident. The other children were on their dragons overhead.

Negus was now coming with his Gurs. F E A R emanated outward in rings from Negus. Shadows tried to grip the children's dragon pearls, and the children called out for their dragon's pearls to come across the ocean waves to where Daniel was. Harry, Jake, and Grandy held the trident between them in mid-flight when the shadows and the flying dragon Gurs hit them full force. There was a ripping tear in the air as one of the Gurs, and then many more, grabbed away the trident and ran to Negus carrying it.

"We can't let them get away," called Daniel to the others, and Alfred answered it was too late. Negus had taken it inside himself with a roar of laughter.

Grandy put herself between Negus and the newly born white pearl.

"Guard the pearl," said Alfred. He swooped down and lifted

Daniel from the water. Lindy's dragon, Sara, did the same. All four pearls were back in the hands of the children.

One giant white pearl like Offoron hovered in the fog that surround it. Negus would be back, thought Daniel.

Where was Grandy going? She was chasing Negus back onto the beach. Using her ring, the one Daniel had always admired, she blasted Negus with a ribbon of fire.

Daniel and the three other children form a box around the pearl, and Negus turned on Grandy and Grandy and her dragon were on the run. Negus was coming yet again. The force of shadow nearly upon them all. Grandy and her dragon were now inside the box the other dragons had formed around the new giant pearl.

The rings…and the dragon's pearls… Alfred said from his soul heart to Daniel.

Daniel took his ring and pointed it to Harry's dragon's pearl and each child did the same. Waves of air pushed past and over and around the children. It was a repelling force field that surrounded all of them and it hit Negus full force like a sonic boom. Everything shuddered.

Negus and his minions could not get inside the field.

Hearts were pounding and the air was still and quiet on the inside of the field.

Negus let out a roar, "I have the trident. I will win, Offoron and Alfred. I will win. We shall see." Negus flew in the opposite direction, laughing.

"Now, children," called Offoron, from inside the pearls. "Look with your left eye into the pearl," and in a wink of time, they were flying not on Zorteck but on Earth. The children were flying over Atlantis.

Offoron was there waiting in a warp of time.

ATLANTIS

19

Offoron waited. He waited for the sight of them flying through the wild winds to the cavernous mouth of Dragon Mountain, the last of Atlantis. He waited for the return of the last Dragon's Pearl like himself. He waited in a time warp.

Seeing the sea below them, they came guiding the pearl into the mouth of Atlantis. Dragon Mountain hovered over them waiting too for something to happen so the rest of Atlantis could be recovered. In some places above water, in other places below water, Atlantis waited for an awakening.

In was dark when they finally arrived and lightning followed the ridge and let them inside. The two pearls were face to face and talking in a language long since dead.

"Offoron."

"Newboron."

The dragons, children, and Grandy gathered around the two pearls that now hovered in the center of the council chambers. Herman was there also with both eyes open.

It was decided then. The two pearls spoke in unison.

"The ruse had worked."

Offoron spoke, "Negus had gone for the trident. Newboron had escaped, and the first part of the plan was in play."

Other dragons were arriving in the chamber until it was nearly full.

Each dragon opened its breastplate and the dragon's pearls that were within were released into the air. The baby pearls spiraled upwards to the egg-shaped dome of the chamber.

Alfred opened his breastplate as well.

Inside Daniel saw a spinning galaxy of light in which the pearls had hovered and now which were also released into the open air.

"Daniel," said Alfred, "Atlantis is composed of many things. I carry the galaxy and others carry other parts of Atlantis inside us. We will join them together once you use you ring to repair the rip in time. But there is great peril to you, Daniel."

Daniel nodded, so did the other children and Grandy.

"We have gathered the pearls like shards of what once was, to create what could be again," said Alfred.

Herman crowed, "But what you fear most Daniel will also come alive and it will consume you." He pointed with his bony finger to Daniel's heart. "If you let it in a little negative will come into being, and the galaxy of Atlantis will be no more. Instead, it will explode outward and off at light speed into the dark it will go. Only you, Daniel, can stop the darkness of Negus."

"But how? I am only a boy. What can I do?"

Alfred replied, "I will help you."

Newboron and Offoron started to shiver and shake and all of a sudden with the force of the wind and a boom like that that was on the beach they had just left, the two pearls combined into one.

The other pearls hovered around the center of the one. Then out of Alfred's breastplate flew a galaxy that stretched itself out, and the baby pearls guided it into place.

There was such awe in the children and in Grandy to see the birth of the universe, the rebirth of Atlantis.

Other things were added. One dragon added a sun; one a cosmic rainbow. Hundreds of things came out and danced in space of and formed to a world including creatures Daniel had never seen before.

A blink of an eye in his pearl and Daniel was back in the water. His dragon's pearl hovering above him.

No Mermaids. There was Daniel now back in the sea water alone, caught in a riptide. It got very very dark. Daniel started to swim for the shore. He wasn't getting any closer to the beach and he was getting tired. There, when he was almost at defeat, he met his Negus.

"You die."

"I will not give in," said Daniel. "You will not win."

Daniel heard Alfred in his soul voice. *Swim at an angle to the shore Daniel. Swim.*

Negus said, "Swim straight. You will get there faster."

Daniel did not know what to do. What Negus was saying made perfect sense in terms of distance, but Daniel was very, very tired.

He wasn't moving forward, but going further out to sea.

His arms trying to hold himself up in the water; his body too heavy to carry.

He had to make a decision.

Daniel heard Alfred speak to him again, *fiery focus, Daniel.*

There was light in his heart that day and again he felt it; felt what Alfred had said to do was somehow right.

Daniel started to swim at an angle to the beach.

Something was happening. It was like everything was awake and alive. With each stroke, Daniel could feel a rip in time being repaired, and Negus as hollering and screaming at him.

Daniel took another stroke and another.

Above him he could see the light of the universe of Atlantis descending from above and taking shape in the ocean.

It was as if Negus, the darkness were unraveling as he took another stroke and another. Daniel was getting closer and closer to the beach.

Finally, near exhaustion, Daniel climbed out of the water and looked out to sea of calm, not riptide.

Negus, what was to left of him, hovered over and around him. It was then, that his ring came alive and spoke of being his shadow guard.

The ring blasted a calm center in the middle of the blackness. Negus howled. It was then that the Gurs struck at him with their fangs. One of the Gurs bit him on the shoulder taking out a chunk of flesh. Daniel howled in agony as the poison from the Gur spread up his arm towards his heart.

And Daniel saw a Gur he recognized. Barth.

Barth was carrying the feather that Daniel had given him such a long time ago. Barth was flying above Daniel waving the feather, telling him he was almost there. "Find the trident. The trident would save you, but you will have to go into the heart of Negus."

The ring flew off of Daniel's finger and with laser focus shot down Gur after Gur, either in flight or coming to the ground. The beach got darker and darker.

Negus growled, "You won't be able to do it. You are nothing...nothing, Dan...iel."

Where dark got darker yet, Daniel pushed through. He was beyond tired now and ached in every bone to the sinew. The chill gripped his being as well as his heart. Then without really understanding how, Daniel's ring returned to him. Like the compass, it lit like a lamp in the darkness. Daniel stumbled forward. He was inside the Negus. One of the baby pearls flew in, Daniel quite by accident took a gulp of air and swallowed it.

Something was happening to Daniel....

Daniel felt something in the darkness. It was cold like metal, and he gripped it in his hands. It was the trident, but something more, heart-stopping dread in what should have been early morning light. He felt again the poison of fear grip his heart from the bite of the Gur, and held the trident to the sky. With a bolt of blue lightning, the trident drained the fear from Daniel. The poison was gone.

"We will meet again Daniel," said a very wicked, wicked voice. "We will meet again. Atlantis will yet be mine," and then the darkness was gone....

The crimson colors dance in yellows, oranges, and blue water, and a dragon flew on wings so free to touch the sun before the light was spun, Alfred arrived. Daniel, you are one of us now. You have become a dragon.

"You have repaired the rip in time and space," said Alfred. "Look at your hands, Daniel."

"What?" Daniel turned and a tail followed him. He saw his own hands and they were not hands anymore. They were talons. He had golden scales all over like Alfred. "Oh, my."

"You now can change into any form you wish."

Daniel awoke after being oh so tired.

"Grandy, Grandy, I had a dream."

"Yes, child...tell me all."

Daniel ran to the metal box with the dragon on it and touched its tail. The tail unlocked the box, and the map unfurled in front of them. He put his hand on the map once more.

The map of the Atlantis illuminated the words 'repaired' and showed a black mass on the move. Negus! The compass flew out of the box and into Daniel's hands and it pointed straight to Dragon Mountain.

"We have to go there now, Grandy."

"Yes, we do."

ABOUT THE AUTHOR

Wendy grew up in an oral tradition family without a dictionary in the house. After grade 12, Wendy went to work for 10 years before going for her university degree in English. There she learned a lot more about literature and found her love for writing.

After graduating from Simon Fraser University, Wendy entered a competition held by the City of New Westminster for Poetry. She won the contest that was judged by the Mayor of the City, Mayor Wright, Don Benson, one of two poet laureates in Canada, and the oldest library in BC. Some of her words have also appeared in the Western News and the Penticton Herald. Both are published in Penticton, BC.

Wendy has another book called, "Scare Away the Dark" which is also available at Amazon.com; however, Dragon's Pearl is her first novelette for kids and kids at heart.

"I hope you enjoyed this book and it is my hope that you tell your friends about it. I would enjoy receiving your stories and pictures by email at wendy@sharpwritingsolutions.com. I will answer you.

"If you would like me to make a series, another story to follow this one, let me know by leaving a review at Amazon.com or Amazon.ca."

Wendy